The NUTCRACKER
A Story of Christmas Magic

This is the story of The Nutcracker. It is a story of romance, adventure, battles, love, and dancing...lots of dancing...beautiful, breathtaking and magical dancing. But mostly, it is a story about the magic of Christmas.

This story starts on Christmas Eve, many years ago, in a land far away, where a young girl named Clara is happily looking forward to her family's big Christmas celebration...

Clara helped her mother prepare everything for the party. The big Christmas tree was wonderfully decorated with all sorts of sparkly ornaments and lights. There were so many candy canes and treats hanging from the tree, Clara thought they could never all be eaten. Clara and her mother made a feast of their favorite Christmas foods for everyone to eat. There was a roaring fire in the fireplace, and Christmas music could be heard throughout the house.

Clara was happy. She loved parties, and she loved Christmas...
and today there were both. Clara was so happy that she even
felt happy to be playing with her little brother, Fritz, and his
toy soldiers.

Soon the guests started to arrive. Everybody was dressed
for a Christmas party, and Clara loved the fancy outfits.
The partygoers were all full of Christmas cheer. They were
laughing and singing Christmas carols, and just having an
all-around great time.

Suddenly, the door burst open. There was Clara's favorite uncle, Uncle Dross. He was dressed in a beautiful Christmas suit and had a big box in his arms. It was all wrapped up in shiny paper and bows. He had helpers with him, and they carried in three more big boxes that were also wrapped up beautifully. The helpers placed the packages with Uncle Dross and then slipped out of the room.

Uncle Dross was a toymaker and always brought wonderful, magical gifts. All the kids were so excited to see what Uncle Dross had brought, they were clapping and jumping up and down. Uncle Dross beckoned Fritz over to help him open one of the big boxes.

Uncle Dross lifted Fritz up high and told him to pull the big
bow on the box. Fritz pulled hard, and suddenly, the front
of the box opened like a door. Out of the box marched the
biggest toy soldier Fritz had ever seen. He was dressed in a
bright red uniform, and he stood tall at attention waiting for
Fritz to command him. Soon Fritz had the soldier marching
about the room with great precision. Fritz was so happy he
was smiling ear-to-ear.

Uncle Dross then invited Clara and her cousin over to help him open the other two big boxes. He lifted them up one-by-one to tug at the big ribbons. When both boxes fell open, the girls stood back to admire the wonderful, big dolls that came tumbling out. It was Harlequin the clown and his clown girlfriend, the beautiful Colombine. Harlequin and Colombine were soon tumbling around the room. They were leaping and jumping, and twirling and dancing, to the pleasure of all who watched. Soon everyone was laughing with joy and clapping for the wonderful clowns.

Finally, for the fourth box, Uncle Dross walked up to Clara, gave her a big hug and announced, "Now, for my goddaughter, Clara, I have brought something very special!" Uncle Dross gave Clara the beautifully wrapped box. When Clara pulled at the ribbon, the box opened and there was a wonderful, strange doll. He was a tall, handsome soldier in full dress uniform, and Clara wondered at the skill and craftsmanship of Uncle Dross's work. She also wondered at the soldier's strange mouth...

Uncle Dross picked up a walnut from a dish on the buffet table and put it in the soldier's mouth. Then he pulled down hard on a lever in the soldier's back. Then he pushed up gently on the same lever. The mouth opened up to reveal the walnut, only now it was cracked open so you could easily enjoy the tasty treat inside. "He's a NUTCRACKER!" exclaimed Uncle Dross. Everyone laughed and clapped.

Clara hugged her new favorite toy and said, "Thank you, Uncle Dross.
I love him! And I love you!" She then gave Uncle Dross a big hug and a kiss.

Uncle Dross whispered in her ear, "Be very careful with him, dear. He is
very special. He is filled to the brim with Christmas magic."

It was getting late and time for bed. As you know yourself, every child has a hard time falling asleep on Christmas Eve, because they are so excited. Tonight, Clara found it nearly impossible. She was so happy with her new Nutcracker that she missed him even though he was just downstairs near the Christmas tree.

It seemed like hours had passed, and Clara just couldn't stop thinking about the Nutcracker. Finally, she decided she would sneak downstairs and get him. She crept lightly down the hall to the top of the stairs. All the lights were out, and she was a little scared. She finally braved her way downstairs and into the family room. There, under the lights of the Christmas tree, her Nutcracker stood at attention. She picked him up, carried him to the couch, and snuggled him into her arms. Quick as a blink...she was sound asleep.

Clara awoke with a start. It was still night, still dark outside, and she was alone in the room. At least she thought she was alone...but then something caught her eye. The toys were moving...the soldiers were marching, led by the Nutcracker...the clowns were dancing about the room...everything was alive! Even more shocking to her, Clara realized she was the same size as the toys! It was like she was one of them.

Suddenly, she jumped. She couldn't believe what she saw sneaking up under the tree. It was the Mouse King dressed in all his kingly attire, holding a sword and leading a mouse army. They were sneaking up on the toy soldiers and were about to attack without warning.

Clara yelled in fear for the toy soldiers,
alerting them to their imminent danger.
The mouse army charged forward, led by
the Mouse King. The Nutcracker rallied
his troops and led a
charge right back.

It was a fierce battle, and for a while it seemed the mouse army might prevail, but the valiant Nutcracker led his toy soldiers with skill. The toy soldiers fought hard, eventually gaining the upper hand and pushing the mouse army back. The Nutcracker found he was locked in a sword fight with the Mouse King, and the two battled fiercely. Clara was filled with concern for her beautiful Nutcracker and was so upset that she pulled off her slipper and threw it at the Mouse King. Her slipper bounced off the Mouse King's crown and distracted him just enough for the Nutcracker to gain the advantage and defeat the Mouse King. When all the other mice saw their fallen King, they ran off in fear carrying the Mouse King with them.

Clara was so excited she ran to the Nutcracker and threw her arms around him. Then she suddenly stepped back and looked again in stunned amazement. Somehow the Nutcracker had become a handsome young prince, and Clara had turned into a beautiful princess in a beautiful gown. The Nutcracker Prince bowed low before her and kissed her hand asking her, "Dear Princess Clara, would you accompany me to my magical land and come visit my marzipan castle?"

Princess Clara smiled and responded, "I would love to, my Nutcracker Prince!" As Princess Clara turned and looked, she realized they were now in a beautiful world of ice and snow with soft, giant snowflakes falling down around them.

The Nutcracker Prince led Princess Clara to his boat, and they sailed down a river of honey. The ice and snow melted away behind them as they traveled to The Land of Sweets & Treats.

After a beautiful sail through this magical land, Princess Clara and the Nutcracker Prince came to a marzipan castle. At the castle, they were greeted by the Sugar Plum Fairy and all her ladies-in-waiting. Princess Clara was in awe. The castle was beautiful, the Sugar Plum Fairy was most beautiful, and the Nutcracker Prince was obviously the prince of all this magical land.

The Sugar Plum Fairy invited them to sit on a magnificent throne and enjoy a feast of the best that The Land of Sweets & Treats had to offer. There was to be a celebration dance in their honor.

The first to dance were the Hot Chocolates. Their outfits were swirling dark chocolate and fluffy whipped cream with marshmallow decorations. They danced the dance of Spanish Fandango Dancers with twirling fun and splashes of sweetness.

Princess Clara clapped
with joy.

Next to dance were the mysterious and dark Arabian Coffees. Mystical and magical, they moved with a graceful elegance.

Princess Clara was entranced by the beauty of their dance and almost cried when their dance ended.

Then the Chinese Tea dancers came out
and performed the happy and playful ritual
of their eastern dance. They twirled,
high-stepped, and seemed to enjoy
dancing so much that Princess Clara
felt like jumping up and dancing
right along.

By the time they had finished,
Princess Clara was exhausted
just from dancing along in
her mind.

After the Chinese Tea Dancers completed their dance, a beautiful Russian babushka doll appeared that twirled and danced to a lilting Russian tune. To Princess Clara's delight, the doll suddenly popped open to let out a slightly smaller doll. The two dolls danced for a moment when, POP!, the new smaller doll popped open to let out a slightly smaller doll! Now there were three dancing dolls until, POP!, it happened again... and again...and again...with every new doll popping open and letting out a smaller doll until there were nine dolls. Each beautiful doll was slightly smaller than the one before it, and they were all dancing and twirling to the music.

It was so magical that Princess Clara nearly fainted from joy.

The dancing went on and on for so long it was as if this one night lasted for many days. Princess Clara realized it was time she should be heading home, but just as she was preparing to go, a handsome cavalier strode into the party and began dancing with the Sugar Plum Fairy. All the ladies-in-waiting and all the other dancers drew back and watched as this stunning two-some danced a dance that would be remembered for generations.

With the conclusion of the dance of the Sugar Plum Fairy, it was now truly time to go. Princess Clara bid all her new friends goodbye and set sail for home. As Princess Clara and her Nutcracker Prince sailed away from The Land of Sweets & Treats, she was both sad to leave and filled with joy for having visited. As the boat gently rocked, she found herself drifting off into the memories of her magical evening...

When Clara woke, it was Christmas morning.
She was back on her couch.
Her Nutcracker was back at attention under the Christmas tree.
Everything was as it had been the night before.

"It was all a dream," she thought...but was it? As Clara sat up on the couch and looked closer at her Nutcracker, he seemed to be smiling...but was he? She wasn't sure...

...She wasn't sure, until she reached into the pocket of her nightgown and found a handful of delicious Sweets & Treats!

THE END